W0010657

9781013477706

CLASSICS
OF
RUSSIAN
LITERATURE

I. GONCHAROV
Drawing by P. Borel
(from the photograph of 1847)

Иван Гончаров

Обыкновенная история

ИЗДАТЕЛЬСТВО ЛИТЕРАТУРЫ НА ИНОСТРАННЫХ ЯЗЫКАХ
Москва

IVAN GONCHAROV

THE SAME OLD STORY

FOREIGN LANGUAGES PUBLISHING HOUSE

Moscow

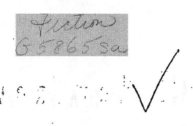

TRANSLATED FROM THE RUSSIAN
BY IVY LITVINOVA

DESIGNED BY V. A. NOSKOV

CONTENTS

PART ONE

One summer day the entire household of Anna Pavlovna Aduyeva, the owner of a modest estate in
the village of Grachi, was up at dawn, from the
mistress herself to Barbos the watchdog.

But Anna Pavlovna's only son, the twenty-year-old
Alexander Fyodorich, slept the sound sleep of youth. The
house was full of fuss and flurry, but everybody went on
tiptoe and spoke in whispers, so as not to wake the young
master. If anyone made the slightest noise, or spoke loudly,
Anna Pavlovna was on the spot instantly, like an infuriat-
ed lionness, scolding the thoughtless one severely, shower-
ing insulting epithets, and sometimes, if very angry and
feeling strong enough, even using her fists.

In the kitchen frantic preparations were on foot, as if
for a great company, although the proprietor's family con-
sisted of only two persons—Anna Pavlovna and Alexander
Fyodorich. In the coach-house the carriage was being pol-
ished and the wheels greased. All were busy, all worked in
the sweat of their brow. Barbos was the only one who had
nothing to do, but even he took part in the general stir in
his own way. When a footman or the coachman passed him,
or a maidservant scurried across the yard, he wagged his tail
and sniffed energetically at the passer-by, while his eyes

seemed to say: I do wish somebody would tell me what all the fuss is about!

Now, all this fuss was simply because Anna Pavlovna was seeing her son off to work in a government office in Petersburg, or, as she put it, to see the world, and let the world see him. A tragic day for her! And that is why she was so melancholy and irritable. Every now and then, in the midst of her cares, she opened her mouth to give some order, but stopped half-way through the sentence, her voice failing her, and turned aside to wipe away a tear, or if too late, to let it drop into the trunk in which she was packing Sashenka's clothes. Tears had long been welling up in her heart, they lay like a weight in her breast, reached her throat and threatened to gush up in torrents. But, as if saving them up for the last farewell, she only shed an occasional tear.

She was not the only one mourning the coming separation— Sashenka's man-servant, Yevsei, was also overcome with grief. He was going with his master to Petersburg, leaving the warmest nook in the house, behind the stove in the room of Agrafena, the prime minister of Anna Pavlovna's cabinet, and what was still more important for Yevsei—her housekeeper.

There was only just room behind the stove for two chairs and a table, for serving tea, coffee, and *hors-d'oeuvres*. Yevsei had entrenched himself firmly both on one of the chairs and in the heart of Agrafena. The second chair was for herself alone.

The affair of Agrafena and Yevsei was an old story in the house. Like all such affairs it was discussed, with much slanderous gossip about the persons involved, and then, like all such affairs, dropped. The mistress herself was used to seeing them together, and they had enjoyed ten years of bliss. There are not many who can count ten happy years in their whole existence. But now the hour of bereavement had struck! Farewell, warm nook, farewell, Agrafena Ivanovna, farewell, games of *duraki* *, coffee, vodka, cordials—farewell everything!

Yevsei sat in his accustomed place, sighing noisily. Agrafena, a perpetual scowl on her face, busied herself about the house. She expressed her grief in a way of her own. That day she poured out the tea fiercely, and instead of handing the first cup, very strong, to her mistress, as she usually did, she poured it away, as if to say "nobody shall have it," taking her mistress's rating with stoical firmness. The coffee was boiled too long, the cream "caught," the cups slipped through her fingers. She did not place the tray on the table, she banged it down. She did not merely unlock cupboards and doors, she wrenched them open. But she shed no tears, only vented her rage on everything and everybody. And this was quite in keeping with her character. She was never satisfied; nothing suited her; she was always scolding and complaining. But at this crucial moment of her life her character displayed itself in all its splendour. And it seemed as if no one annoyed her so much as Yevsei.

"Agrafena Ivanovna!" he wailed with a plaintive tenderness that did not quite suit his tall, but closely-knit figure.

"Couldn't you sit somewhere else, you dolt?" she replied, as if he had never sat there before. "Let me pass, I want to get a towel."

"Ah, Agrafena Ivanovna!" he repeated languidly, sighing and getting up, only to sink back on to the seat as soon as she had taken the towel.

"He can do nothing but whimper! Sticking to me like a leech! A perfect pest, dear Lord!"

And she dropped a spoon noisily into the slop-basin.

---

* A card-game, something like "Beggar My Neighbour."— *Tr.*

"Agrafena!", came suddenly from the next room. "Have you gone mad? Don't you know Sashenka's still asleep? What are you doing—fighting with your beloved, by way of farewell?"

"You'd like me not to stir, sit there like the dead!" hissed Agrafena venomously, drying a cup with both her hands as if she would have liked to break it into pieces.

"Farewell! Farewell!" said Yevsei, heaving a mighty sigh. "The last day, Agrafena Ivanovna!"

"And thank God for that! Good riddance to bad rubbish! There'll be more room. Get out of the way, now, I can't move! Stretching out your long legs!"

He tried touching her on the shoulder—and didn't she give him what for! He heaved another sigh, but made no attempt to move. And he was quite right, that was not what Agrafena wanted. Yevsei knew this, and was not disturbed.

"Who will sit in my place?" he murmured, with another sigh.

"A pixie!" she snapped.

"God grant it! So long as it's not Proshka. And who will play *duraki* with you?"

"Well, and supposing Proshka does, what of it?" she asked venomously.

Yevsei rose.

"Don't play with Proshka—only not that!" he said in anxious, almost threatening tones.

"And who's to prevent me, pray? The likes of you?"

"Dear Agrafena Ivanovna!" he pleaded, putting his arm round what might have been called her waist, if there had been the slightest hint of a waist in her figure.

She responded to the embrace by sticking her elbow into his chest.

"Dear Agrafena Ivanovna!" he repeated. "Will Proshka love you as much as I do? You know what a rascal he is—

14

he's after every woman he sees. And I—oh! Why, you're the apple of my eye! If it weren't the mistress's will ... oh!"

He groaned and made a gesture of despair. Agrafena could bear no more—at last even *her* grief showed itself in tears.

"Can't you leave me alone, you miserable wretch?" she said through her tears. "How you do go on! As if I would take up with Proshka! Can't you see nobody can get a word of sense out of him? All he thinks about is pawing me...."

"So he *has* been after you! The scoundrel! And you never told me a word! I'd—"

"Only let him try to touch me! As if I was the only female in the house! Me to take up with Proshka! What next, I wonder! It makes me sick even to sit next to him—the dirty swine. If one doesn't look out he's up to striking someone, or eating the mistress's victuals under one's very nose, and nobody ever noticing!"

"Agrafena Ivanovna, if the necessity *should* arise—the Evil One is very cunning—better let Grishka take my place. He's a quiet, hard-working chap, he isn't one of your scoffers."

"There you go again!" shouted Agrafena. "What makes you shove all sorts of people on me—as if I was some— Get out! There's plenty of you men, and I'm not the one to throw myself at the first-comer. You were the only one, you pixie, I got myself mixed up with, the Evil One must have caught me in his toils for my sins, and I repent it ... and you keep on nagging at me!"

"God reward you for your goodness! It's a weight off my shoulders!" exclaimed Yevsei.

"Now he's pleased!" she shouted ferociously. "If you find anything to be pleased about in that you're welcome to it!"

And her very lips turned pale with fury. Neither of them spoke for a few moments.

And then: "Agrafena Ivanovna," began Yevsei timidly.

15

"Now what?"

"I was almost forgetting—I haven't had a crumb since the morning."

"Is that all?"

"It's on account of my grief."

She reached for a glass of vodka and two huge hunks of bread and ham from behind a sugar-loaf on the bottom shelf of the cupboard. All this had long been made ready for him by her solicitous hands. She thrust the food and drink at him—you would hardly fling food to a dog so roughly. One hunk fell on the floor.

"Here you are—choke yourself! The devil take you! Quiet now, the whole house can hear you champing!"

She turned away from him with an expression of assumed disgust, and he began slowly eating, eyeing Agrafena from beneath his brows, and covering his mouth with his free hand.

In the meanwhile a carriage and three drove up to the gate. The shaft-bow was fixed over the wheel-horse. The little bell, hanging from it, its clapper lolling from side to side, emitted hollow sounds, like the tongue of a drunken man, bound and flung into a cell. The coachman tied up the horses under a pent-house, took off his cap, and extracted from it a grubby towel, with which he proceeded to wipe the sweat from his face. Catching sight of him from the window, Anna Pavlovna turned pale. Her knees gave, and her hands hung limp at her sides, although she had been on the look-out for the carriage. Mastering her emotion, she called Agrafena.

"Go on tiptoe, very, very quietly, and see if Sashenka's still asleep," she said. "His last day will go in sleep, the darling, and I shan't be able to look my fill at him. But no, you can't—you'd steal in about as quietly as a cow. I'd better go myself."

16

And off she went.

"Go yourself, since you're not a cow," muttered Agrafena, returning to her room. "So I'm a cow, am I? You haven't many cows like me, have you?"

Anna Pavlovna was met by Alexander himself, a strong, healthy, flaxen-haired lad in the hey-day of youth. He greeted his mother cheerfully, but catching sight of the trunks and bundles turned in silent embarrassment to the window and began tracing on the pane with his finger. A moment later he was talking to his mother again, and even regarding the preparations for the journey with carefree enjoyment.

"You shouldn't have slept so late, my love!" said Anna Pavlovna. "Your face is all puffy. Let me rinse your eyes and cheeks with rose-water."

"Please don't, Mamma."

"What would you like for breakfast—will you begin with tea or coffee? I've ordered chopped meat fried in sour cream. Will you have some?"

"Anything you like, Mamma."

Anna Pavlovna went on packing the linen for a while, and then stopped, gazing wistfully at her son.

"Sasha," she said, after a short pause.

"What is it, Mamma?"

She hesitated, as if in vague terror.

"Where are you going, my love, why are you going?" she brought out softly, at last.

"Where, Mamma? Why, to Petersburg, to ... to —"

"Listen, Sasha," she said, in agitated tones, placing a hand on his shoulder, with the evident intention of making one last attempt. "It's not too late—think it over! Don't go!"

"Not go? Impossible! Besides, the ... the clothes are all packed," he said, at a loss for words.

"Your clothes! There, and there, and there ... look—
they're not packed."

She emptied the trunk in three armfuls.

"But, Mamma, what d'you mean? I'm all ready, and now
you want me to stay. What would people think?"

He looked unhappy.

"It's not for myself—it's for your sake. What are you going
for? To seek happiness? Aren't you happy here? Doesn't
your mother think all day long how to satisfy your light-
est whim? Of course you are of an age when your mother's
efforts to please you are not enough to make you happy.
And I don't expect them to. But, look around you—everyone wants to please you. Marya Karpovna's daughter,
Sonyushka, too. Ah, you're blushing? How she loves you, God
bless her, the darling! They say she hasn't slept for three
nights!"

"Come now, Mamma! She only— "

"As if I couldn't see! Oh—I mustn't forget! She promised
to hem some handkerchiefs for you. 'I'll do them all myself,'
she said. 'I won't let anyone else do them, and I'll mark
them, too.' What more could you wish? Don't go!"

He listened in silence, with bowed head, playing with the
tassels of his dressing-gown.

"What will you find in Petersburg?" she continued. "Do
you think you'll be as well looked after as you are here?
Oh, my dear! God knows what you'll have to endure—cold
and hunger and want—you'll have to bear it all. There are
plenty of bad people everywhere, but you won't find good
people so easily. And as for distinction—what's the differ-
ence whether it's town or country? When you know nothing
of Petersburg life you think you are the first person in the
world, living here. It's the same everywhere, dearie! You're
well-bred and clever and handsome. The only joy left to an
old woman like me is to look at you. You could marry, God

would send you little ones, and I could dandle them—and you would have no sorrows or cares, you could live out your days in peace and quiet, envying no one. Perhaps things won't be so good there, perhaps you'll remember my words.... Do stay, Sashenka!"

He cleared his throat and sighed, but uttered not a word.

"See!" she continued, opening the balcony door. "Can you bear to leave such a sweet nook?"

A cool fragrance came into the room through the open door. A garden planted with ancient lime-trees, dense thickets of wild rose, wild cherry trees and lilac bushes stretched from the house far into the distance. There were beds of gaily-coloured flowers among the trees, paths running in all directions; and beyond them lay the lake, softly splashing against its shores; one half of it, smooth as a mirror, reflected the gold of the morning sun, the surface of the other half was ruffled and of a deep blue, like the sky above it. Still further, the tossing, multicoloured cornfields rose in a kind of amphitheatre towards the dark woods in the background.

Anna Pavlovna, shading her eyes from the sun with one hand, pointed to all these objects in turn with her free hand.

"See," she said, "how beautifully God has adorned our fields! We shall take as much as twelve hundred poods of rye alone from these fields. And over there are wheat and buckwheat. The buckwheat is not as good as it was last year, probably the harvest will be poor. But look at the woods— see how they have grown! See how great is God's wisdom! We will get at the very least a thousand rubles for our wood. And the game—the game! And it's all yours, dear son. I am only your stewardess. Just look at that lake—what splendour! Truly divine! And the fish in it! The only fish we have to buy is sturgeon—the lake is teeming with ruff,

perch and crucian—enough for ourselves and our servants.
Look at your cows and horses grazing over there!You are the
master of everything here, while there—who knows—everyone will lord it over you. And you want to run away from
all this bliss—whither to, you don't rightly know yourself,
perhaps—God forbid!—you'll land in some swamp. Stay!"

He said nothing.

"You're not listening," she said. "What's that you're
staring at?"

He pointed in silent thoughtfulness to the distance. Anna
Pavlovna followed his glance, and changed countenance.
Between the fields the road wound like a snake, disappear-
ing into the woods and reappearing on the other side—the
road to the Promised Land, to Petersburg. Anna Pavlovna
was silent a few minutes, trying to master her emotions.

"So that's it," she at last brought out mournfully. "Well,
never mind, my love! Go, since you long to leave this place,
I will not keep you. You shall never say that your mother
spoiled your youth and your prospects."

Unhappy mother! This is the reward for all your love!
Is this what you expected? Ah, but mothers expect no reward. A mother loves unthinkingly, disinterestedly. If
you are great, famous, handsome, proud, if your name is on
the lips of all men, if your deeds are renowned throughout
the world—the old woman quivers with joy, she weeps,
laughs, prays long and fervently. And her son seldom thinks
of sharing his fame with his mother. If you are low-spirited
and dull-witted, if you are poor in soul or body, if Nature
has set the brand of ugliness upon you, if you are sick, body
or soul, if, finally, men repulse you and you find no place
among them—all the more readily will you find a place in
your mother's heart. She presses the ill-favoured, misbegot-
ten offspring still more warmly to her breast, prays still
longer and more fervently for him.

Must Alexander be considered callous because he brought himself to part with his mother? He was twenty years of age. Life had smiled on him from the cradle.

His mother had petted and spoiled him, as mothers always do spoil an only child. His nurse had sung to him while he was still in his cradle that he would always be rich and never know sorrow. His professors had declared he would go far, and when he returned home from his studies the neighbour's daughter had smiled at him. Even Vaska, the old tomcat, seemed to prefer him to everyone else in the house.

Of grief, tears and disasters he knew only by hearsay, as people know of some disease which has never come their way, and only lurks remotely among less fortunate folk. And so the future presented itself to him in rainbow colours. Something seemed to beckon him from afar, though what it was he did not exactly know. Delightful visions flitted by before he could make out what they were. Blended sounds rang in his ears—the voice of glory, the voice of love. And all this kept him in a state of delicious agitation.

His home soon became too narrow for him. Nature, the love of his mother, the adoration of his nurse and the whole household, his soft couch, the good food and the purring of Vaska—all these blessings which are so much appreciated on the downward slope of life, he cheerfully surrendered for an unknown full of irresistible, mysterious charm. Not even the love of Sophia—first love, so tender and rosy—could hold him back. What did he care for it? What he dreamed of was a great passion knowing no limits and capable of resounding feats. In the meantime he loved Sophia with a moderate love while waiting for some great passion to come his way. He dreamed, too, of the services he would do for his country. He had studied diligently and extensively. His diploma testified to his knowledge of a dozen subjects, as well as half a dozen languages, ancient and modern. His fondest dream was to become a famous writer. His verses had astonished his friends. Innumerable paths lay before him, each more alluring than the other. He did not know which to set foot upon. Only the straight road was hidden from his eyes—if he had noticed it, perhaps he would not have gone away. But how could he stay at home? His mother desired it, and that was but natural of course. Love for her son was the only feeling left in her heart, and it seized eagerly upon this last object. But for this, what would there have been left for her to do? She might as well have been dead. It has long ago been pointed out that the heart of a woman cannot exist without love.

. Home life had spoilt Alexander, but it had not corrupted his heart. Nature had done so well by him, that the love of his mother and the adoration of those surrounding him had only affected the better side of his character, developing in him emotional susceptibility, and implanting in him an excessive trustfulness. Perhaps they were the cause of the first stirrings of vanity in him; but vanity itself is a mere mold, everything depends on the material we pour into it.

. Much more unfortunate for him was his mother's inability, for all her tenderness, to instil in him a right attitude to life, to prepare him for the struggle which lay in wait for him, as for everyone. But this would have required a skilled touch, a subtle mind and a great store of experience, not limited by the cramped horizon of rural life. For this she should have loved him less, not thought of him every moment of the day, not shielded him from every care and unpleasantness, not done his weeping and suffering for him when he was a child, so as to keep away from him the approach of storms, she should have let him cope with them himself and think over his own destiny—in a word realize that he was a man. But how was Anna Pavlovna to understand all this—let alone to fulfil these requirements? The reader has

CPSIA information can be obtained
at www.ICGtesting.com
Printed in the USA
BVHW021504090223
658189BV00003BA/114